Golden Retrievers

Stephanie Finne

**Checkerboard
Library**

An Imprint of Abdo Publishing
www.abdopublishing.com

www.abdopublishing.com

Published by Abdo Publishing, a division of ABDO, PO Box 398166, Minneapolis, MN 55439.
Copyright © 2015 by Abdo Consulting Group, Inc. International copyrights reserved in all
countries. No part of this book may be reproduced in any form without written permission from
the publisher. Checkerboard Library™ is a trademark and logo of Abdo Publishing.

Printed in the United States of America, North Mankato, Minnesota.
102014
012015

THIS BOOK CONTAINS
RECYCLED MATERIALS

Cover Photo: iStockphoto
Interior Photos: Corbis pp. 9, 21; iStockphoto pp. 1, 5, 7, 11, 13, 15, 17, 19

Series Coordinator: Tamara L. Britton
Editors: Megan M. Gunderson, Bridget O'Brien
Production: Jillian O'Brien

Library of Congress Cataloging-in-Publication Data

Finne, Stephanie, author.
  Golden retrievers / Stephanie Finne.
      pages cm. -- (Dogs)
  Audience: Ages 8-12.
  Includes index.
  ISBN 978-1-62403-675-0
1. Golden retriever--Juvenile literature. I. Title.
  SF429.G63F56 2015
  636.752'7--dc23
                              2014025408

Contents

The Dog Family

Dogs come in many shapes and sizes. Yet, all dogs belong to the family **Canidae**. The name comes from the Latin word for "dog," which is *canis*.

The first dogs were **domesticated** just over 12,000 years ago. Early humans watched gray wolves hunt together. They wanted to use these wild animals' skills to help them hunt. So, they adopted wolf pups and trained them to be hunting dogs.

Soon humans began **breeding** dogs to do other jobs. Some herded livestock. Others were guard dogs. Some hunting dogs were bred to improve specific hunting skills.

Today, there are more than 400 dog breeds. One of these is the golden retriever. This hunting dog was developed to retrieve waterfowl game birds.

The golden retriever

Golden Retrievers

In the 1800s, an English sportsman named Dudley Marjoribanks **bred** many animals. One day, he met a man who had a golden-coated retriever that had been born in a **litter** of black puppies. The yellow puppy was named Nous. In 1865, Marjoribanks bought the puppy and brought it to his home in Scotland.

Marjoribanks bred Nous with a tweed water spaniel named Belle. Several yellow puppies were born. Over time, Marjoribanks bred them with other tweed water spaniels, wavy-coated retrievers, and red setters. These dogs became the basis for the yellow retriever.

The yellow retriever was first shown in England in 1908 in the flat-coated retriever group. Five years later, the dogs gained separate recognition.

The **American Kennel Club (AKC)** registered the first golden retriever in 1925 in the retriever group. Seven years later, the AKC recognized golden retrievers, or goldens, as a separate **breed**.

The golden retriever is the third most popular breed in the United States.

What They're Like

Golden retrievers are sensitive, loving dogs. They want to be with their people, including children. They are good with other dogs, too. Golden retrievers do not make good watchdogs. They may bark at strangers, but they will quickly warm up to them!

These dogs were **bred** to wait for their owner to give commands. So, they need an owner who is able to train them and give them attention. They are considered "soft" dogs. This means it is best to avoid shouting at or scolding these sensitive dogs.

Goldens are energetic! They need exercise every day. If they don't get enough exercise, they can get into trouble. This can include a lot of unwanted chewing. These dogs were bred to bring a duck or goose to a hunter without damaging it. They use their mouth as a "fifth paw."

Goldens are loyal companions. They need to bond with at least one family member. A devoted golden retriever can be a wonderful addition to your family.

Golden retrievers have a soft mouth. This is a measure of the pressure a dog uses to hold a bird in its mouth. A dog with a soft mouth will not damage the bird.

Coat and Color

Golden retrievers have a beautiful double coat. The **dense** outer coat resists water. A thicker **undercoat** keeps the golden warm while it works outside in harsh weather. The coat can be wavy or straight. It should have a medium texture, rather than being coarse or silky.

The fur on the head, the paws, and the front of the legs is short. The coat is **feathered** on the back of the legs and on the tail. The chest should have longer hair in a **ruff**.

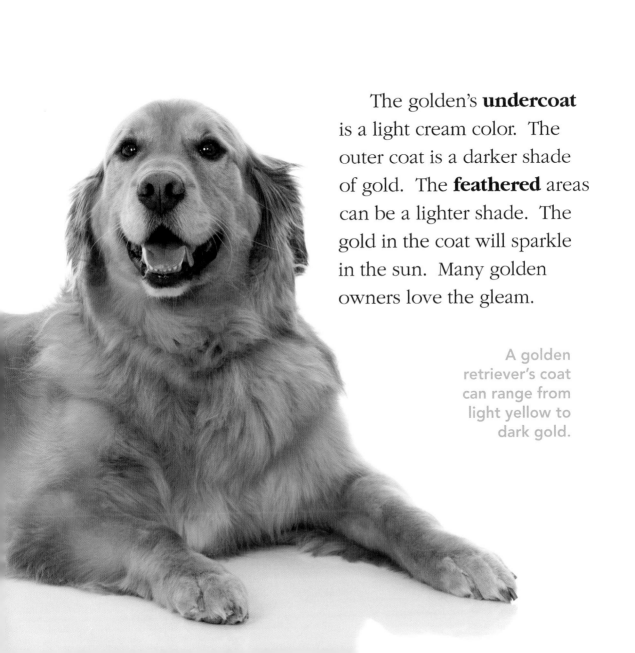

The golden's **undercoat** is a light cream color. The outer coat is a darker shade of gold. The **feathered** areas can be a lighter shade. The gold in the coat will sparkle in the sun. Many golden owners love the gleam.

A golden retriever's coat can range from light yellow to dark gold.

Size

Golden retrievers are medium-sized dogs. Females are 21.5 to 22.5 inches (55 to 57 cm) tall. They are usually about 55 to 65 pounds (25 to 29 kg). Males are slightly larger. They are 23 to 24 inches (58 to 61 cm) tall. They weigh 65 to 75 pounds (29 to 34 kg).

The golden's striking appearance makes it hard to forget! Medium-sized brown eyes sit well apart on a broad head. The ears sit even with the eyes and fall forward close to the dog's cheek. A straight **muzzle** is tipped with a black or brown-black nose.

The **breed**'s medium-long neck leads to its straight, level back. Most of the golden's body is rib cage. Strong, straight legs end in round, webbed paws that help the dog swim. The **feathered** tail is strong and muscular and helps the dog stay balanced in the water.

The visual fields of a golden's two eyes overlap. This is called binocular vision. It allows better depth perception so the dog can quickly locate fallen birds.

Golden retrievers have solid bodies, big feet, and thick necks. They are not delicate dogs! Their strength and beauty are a sight to see.

Care

    Golden retrievers are subject to **hip dysplasia** and heart disease. To make sure your golden is healthy, it will need regular checkups with a veterinarian. The dog will receive an exam and **vaccines** at the visit. The vet can **spay** or **neuter** your dog as well.

    Owners love the golden's full coat. But they must commit to brushing it one to three times a week. Goldens lose hair all of the time. The hair gets trapped in the thick coat. Regular brushing is needed to avoid tangles and **mats**.

Goldens will need more frequent brushing during **shedding** season!

Dental care is very important to a dog's health. Brush your golden's teeth every day. This will prevent tooth decay and gum disease.

This **breed** can adapt to any **environment**. They can live in the city or the country. As long as golden retrievers get exercise and love, they will be happy!

A golden will need regular care for its lifetime. So, its relationship with its doctor will be an important one.

Feeding

Golden retrievers should be fed once or twice a day. These dogs will overeat. So, it is important to watch how much they eat. Do not leave food available at all times. Ask your vet for recommendations on the best food and feeding options for your golden.

All dogs need a balanced diet to be healthy. There are many brands of dog food to choose from. The best option is one labeled "complete and balanced." These dog foods contain enough **protein** and all of the other **nutrients** your dog needs.

Dry dog foods are the most popular type of food. There are also semimoist foods and canned dog food. Semimoist foods contain sugar. Canned food includes excess water. No matter which type you choose, make sure the first three ingredients are a type of protein.

The athletic golden should be a lean dog. Excess weight can aggravate hip dysplasia.

Don't let your golden go thirsty! Water is important for good health. Give the dog fresh water every day. Washing the food and water bowls regularly will also keep your dog healthy.

Things They Need

At home, your golden will need a few supplies. A golden retriever will need its own bed. It will also enjoy a crate to sleep in. The crate will become a comfortable den for your dog.

You will also need grooming tools to care for your golden and its coat. Toenail clippers, dog shampoo for bath time, and combs and brushes are a good start.

All dogs need a collar with an identification tag. If your golden gets lost, an ID tag will provide a way for you to be contacted. A vet can also insert a **microchip** in your new pet. The chip will help identify your pet.

You will need a leash when walking your dog. There are several types of collars and harnesses. You can ask your vet what type is best for your golden retriever.

The golden was **bred** to use its mouth as a tool. So, these dogs enjoy carrying things in their mouths. Leaving chew toys and ropes around so they can pick them up whenever they need to will help keep them content.

A thick bed will reduce stress on a golden's hips and elbows.

Puppies

After mating, a female golden is **pregnant** for about 63 days. When the puppies are born, they cannot see or hear. They are unable to walk. They depend on their mother for everything.

The puppies will drink their mother's milk. Though they cannot see or hear yet, they are able to find their mother to eat. At two weeks old, a puppy's eyes begin to open. Two weeks later, the puppy can see, hear, and play.

When they are eight weeks old, the puppies are old enough to leave their mother. If your family wants to adopt a golden retriever, find a respectable **breeder**. A good breeder will make sure the puppy has had its shots and is healthy. He or she can tell you the health risks of the puppies.

An average litter is about eight puppies.

Golden retriever puppies learn quickly. Around the time they come home with you, they are ready for some basic training. It is important to train and **socialize** your new friend. With training, your golden retriever will be a loving member of your family for 10 to 13 years.

Glossary

American Kennel Club (AKC) - an organization that studies and promotes interest in purebred dogs.

breed - a group of animals sharing the same ancestors and appearance. A breeder is a person who raises animals. Raising animals is often called breeding them.

Canidae (KAN-uh-dee) - the scientific Latin name for the dog family. Members of this family are called canids. They include wolves, jackals, foxes, coyotes, and domestic dogs.

dense - thick or compact.

domesticate - to adapt something to life with humans.

environment - all the surroundings that affect the growth and well-being of a living thing.

feathered - having a fringe of hair.

hip dysplasia (HIHP dihs-PLAY-zhuh) - unusual formation of the hip joint.

litter - all of the puppies born at one time to a mother dog.

mat - a tangled mass.

microchip - an electronic circuit placed under an animal's skin. A microchip contains identifying information that can be read by a scanner.

muzzle - an animal's nose and jaws.

neuter (NOO-tuhr) - to remove a male animal's reproductive glands.

nutrient - a substance found in food and used in the body. It promotes growth, maintenance, and repair.

pregnant - having one or more babies growing within the body.

protein - a substance which provides energy to the body and serves as a major class of foods for animals. Foods high in protein include cheese, eggs, fish, meat, and milk.

ruff - long hair that grows on the neck of an animal.

shed - to cast off hair, feathers, skin, or other coverings or parts by a natural process.

socialize - to adapt an animal to behaving properly around people or other animals in various settings.

spay - to remove a female animal's reproductive organs.

undercoat - short hair or fur partly covered by longer protective fur.

vaccine (vak-SEEN) - a shot given to prevent illness or disease.

Websites

To learn more about Dogs, visit **booklinks.abdopublishing.com**. These links are routinely monitored and updated to provide the most current information available.

Index